THE MIRACLE TREE

I love you much!

So ~~signature~~

Austin Highsmith Garces

D1205530

The Miracle Tree
by Austin Highsmith Garces

Copyright ©2018 by Austin Highsmith Garces

Published by
Doce Blant Publishing, Federal Way, WA
www.doceblantpublishing.com

Illustrations by Austin Highsmith Garces
Cover Design by Fiona Jayde Media

Hardbound ISBN-13: 978-1-7337574-0-9
Paperback ISBN-13: 978-1-7337574-2-3
Digital ISBN-13: 978-1-7337574-1-6

Library of Congress Control Number 2019935217

Printed in the United States of America
www.doceblant.com

It was a normal, but very cold, day on December 21, 1983, in Winston-Salem, North Carolina. It was the Wednesday before Christmas. Dawn dropped off her 5-year-old son, Adam, and 2-year-old daughter, Austin, at the babysitter and then went to her job as a school teacher. Austin really liked playing with her babysitter.

When Austin woke up from her nap at the babysitter, her left eye was swollen shut and very purple. Austin's babysitter knew something was wrong and called Dawn at work. Austin couldn't open her left eye, and she became upset and confused.

Dawn rushed from work to get Austin and Adam. Dawn was very worried and called Austin's dad, Johnny. Johnny worked at a bank. Dawn said she was taking Austin to the doctor.

At the doctor's office, they told Dawn it was very serious and that Austin needed to go to the hospital. Johnny said he would meet them there.

3

They took Austin to the Hospital. At the hospital, the nurses and doctors told Johnny and Dawn that Austin was very sick and would need emergency surgery as soon as possible. They would do surgery and try to remove the infection that was behind her eye. Dawn could tell Austin was nervous. She told Austin that an infection was a sickness, and that the doctors would put her to sleep, then take the sickness out.

Many people came in and out of Austin's hospital room. She learned that her doctor would do her surgery and that the nurses helped the doctor. The nurses also helped with her IV and took her temperature. Her IV would give her medicine while she was sleeping or tired.

5

Dawn and Johnny were very worried for their little girl. Her older brother, Adam, was scared for his little sister. When the doctors spoke with Johnny and Dawn, they told them how serious the surgery and recovery would be, and Austin's parents became very sad. Austin knew she would have to be brave.

Austin's daddy, Johnny, needed to take a walk because he was so sad. He walked down to the Christmas tree that was in the big glass entryway of the hospital.

The Christmas tree was very big and beautiful and covered in ornaments. Johnny did the only thing that he knew to do. He got down on his knees and started to pray. He prayed and prayed over his daughter.

Johnny prayed and asked God to save his daughter's life. He promised that if God saved his daughter's life this Christmas, that he, Dawn, Adam, and Austin would return to this same Christmas tree every year to thank God for saving Austin's life.

A very large male nurse came in to get tiny Austin ready for surgery. When he put his hands on her arm to start to give her the IV, Austin perked up and told the big nurse, "You get you hands offa me!" They all laughed. Austin sure had a lot of spunk!

10

Austin's surgeon was very good at his job. He performed a surgery on Austin, and it was successful, but she would need to stay in the hospital for many days, maybe weeks, following her surgery. She would have to take lots of naps and wear a bandage on her face for a while. Austin said, "I look like a pirate!"

This meant she would be in the hospital over Christmas. So her parents made sure Santa found out where she would be so that she would still wake up to fun presents from Santa on Christmas morning.

On Christmas morning, Austin awakened to many gifts waiting for her at the foot of her hospital bed. Santa brought her a fun baby doll with a bottle to feed her. Austin loved baby dolls, so this made her very happy.

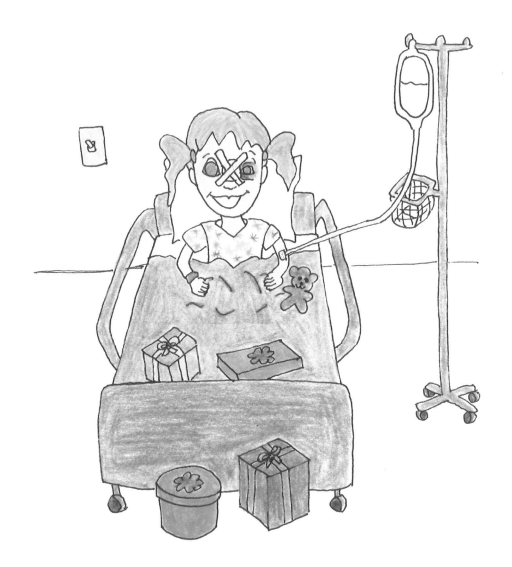

Johnny took Austin for rides around the hospital in her little wheelchair. He even wheeled her down to visit the special Christmas tree where he had prayed. Austin loved it when her daddy took her on races around the hospital in the chair with wheels! She also loved the big, beautiful Christmas tree and all the ornaments.

Austin finally got to go home from the hospital in early January. She still had some side effects from the surgery and sickness. Her big brother, Adam, was so sweet to her and helped take care of her in the mornings. Austin loved her big brother.

That next Christmas, Johnny, Dawn, Adam, and Austin all went back to the special Christmas tree and prayed together as a family.

They did the same thing the year
after that, and the year after that.

The next year, Dawn gave birth to another baby boy. So that Christmas, the baby went to the special Christmas tree with them, too.

Over the years, as they all grew older, the family never forgot to visit the special Christmas tree to say, "thank You" to God for saving Austin's life all those years ago.

In 2017, the whole family visited the tree once again. Austin and Adam were both married, and Adam's daughter was the same age that Austin was when they spent their first Christmas at this hospital with this tree.

In all these years, though they may not have all been able to come every year, Austin's dad, Johnny, never missed a single year. He loved his little girl so much. His love for her and his prayers for her made visiting the special Christmas tree one of their favorite family traditions.

So they will be back next year, and the year after that, and the year after that. Austin hopes one day to have a family of her own. She hopes to bring them back to the special Christmas tree, too, so that she can tell them how much her father, and her Heavenly father, loved her that Christmas, so many years ago.

ABOUT THE STORY

This book is based on the true story of what Austin Highsmith Garces went through as a child. When she was two years old, she was diagnosed with post-orbital cellulitis and was given only a 50-50 chance of survival. In the 35 years since, at least two members of the Highsmith family have visited the Special Christmas Tree at the hospital every year to pray, and to say, "Thank You" to God for saving her life on that cold Christmas in 1983.

ABOUT THE AUTHOR

Austin Highsmith Garces is an actress/producer/writer born in Winston-Salem, NC. She now lives in Los Angeles, CA. Sharing the story about her childhood illness is important to her because she has been afforded the opportunity to visit children at John Hopkins All Children's Hospital in Tampa, FL. There, she felt a connection with the children's journeys. She wanted the children there, and in the hospital that saved her life, to see themselves in her story and find hope for a great life, in spite of their current hardships.

Austin currently lives in L.A. with her husband, Teddy Garces, and hopes to continue telling stories to inspire children and their parents.

For more information about
The Miracle Tree Foundation, visit the website:

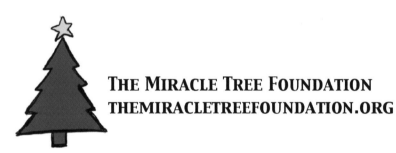

THE MIRACLE TREE FOUNDATION
THEMIRACLETREEFOUNDATION.ORG

CPSIA information can be obtained at www.ICGtesting.com
Printed in the USA
BVIW120512250619
551682BV00008BA/2